THE TOMB
OF SARAH

THE TOMB OF SARAH

FREDERICK GEORGE LORING

WILDSIDE PRESS

Published by Wildside Press LLC.
www.wildsidebooks.com

THE TOMB OF SARAH

My father was the head of a celebrated firm of church restorers and decorators about sixty years ago. He took a keen interest in his work, and made an especial study of any old legends or family histories that came under his observation. He was necessarily very well read and thoroughly well posted in all questions of folklore and medieval legend. As he kept a careful record of every case he investigated the manuscripts he left at his death have a special interest. From amongst them I have selected the following, as being a particularly weird and extraordinary experience. In presenting it to the public I feel it is superfluous to apologize for its supernatural character.

MY FATHER'S DIARY

1841.—*June 17th*. Received a commission from my old friend Peter Grant to enlarge and restore the chancel of his church at Hagarstone, in the wilds of the West Country.

July 5th. Went down to Hagarstone with my head man, Somers. A very long and tiring journey.

July 7th. Got the work well started. The old church is one of special interest to the antiquarian, and I shall endeavour while restoring it to alter the existing arrangements as little as possible. One large tomb, however, must be moved bodily ten feet at least to the southward. Curiously enough, there is a somewhat forbidding inscription upon it in Latin, and I am sorry that this particular tomb should have to be moved. It stands amongst the graves of the Kenyons, an old family which has been extinct in these parts for centuries. The inscription on it runs thus:

SARAH.
1630.

**FOR THE SAKE OF THE DEAD AND THE
WELFARE OF THE LIVING, LET THIS
SEPULCHRE REMAIN UNTOUCHED
AND ITS OCCUPANT UNDISTURBED
TILL THE COMING OF CHRIST.**

**IN THE NAME OF THE FATHER,
THE SON, AND THE HOLY GHOST.**

July 8th. Took counsel with Grant concerning the "Sarah Tomb." We are both very loth to disturb it, but the ground has sunk so beneath it that the safety of the church is in danger; thus we have no choice. However, the work shall be done as reverently as possible under our own direction.

Grant says there is a legend in the neighbourhood that it is the tomb of the last of the Kenyons, the evil Countess Sarah, who was murdered in 1630. She lived quite alone in the old castle, whose ruins still stand three miles from here on the road to Bristol. Her reputation was an evil one even for those days. She was a witch or were-woman, the only companion of her solitude being a familiar in the shape of a huge Asiatic wolf. This creature was reputed to seize upon children, or failing these, sheep and other small animals, and convey them to the castle, where the Countess used to suck their blood. It was popularly supposed that she could never be killed. This, however, proved a fallacy, since she was strangled one day by a mad peasant woman who had lost two children, she declaring that they had both been seized and carried off by the Countess's familiar. This is a very interesting story, since it points to a local superstition very similar to that of the Vampire, existing in Slavonic and Hungarian Europe.

The tomb is built of black marble, surmounted by an enormous slab of the same material. On the slab is a magnificent group of figures. A young and handsome woman reclines upon a couch; round her neck is a piece of rope, the end of which she holds in her hand. At her side is a gigantic dog with bared fangs and lolling tongue. The face of the reclining figure is a cruel one: the corners of the mouth are curiously lifted, showing the sharp points of long canine or dog teeth. The whole group, though magnificently executed, leaves a most unpleasant sensation.

If we move the tomb it will have to be done in two pieces, the covering slab first and then the tomb proper. We have decided to remove the covering slab tomorrow.

July 9th. 6 p.m. A very strange day.

By noon everything was ready for lifting off the covering stone, and after the men's dinner we started the jacks and pulleys. The slab lifted easily enough, though if fitted closely into its seat and was further secured by some sort of mortar or putty, which must have kept the interior perfectly air-tight.

None of us were prepared for the horrible rush of foul, mouldy air that escaped as the cover lifted clear of its seating. And the contents that gradually came into view were more startling still. There lay the fully dressed body of a woman, wizened and shrunk and ghastly pale as if from starvation. Round her neck was a loose cord, and, judging by the scars still visible, the story of death of strangulation was true enough.

The most horrible part, however, was the extraordinary freshness of the body. Except for the appearance of starvation, life might have been only just extinct. The flesh was soft and white, the eyes were wide open and seemed to stare at us with a fearful understanding in them. The body itself lay on mould, without any pretence to coffin or shell.

For several moments we gazed with horrible curiosity, and then it became too much for my workmen, who implored us to replace the covering slab. That, of course, we would not do; but I set the carpenters to work at once to make a temporary cover while we moved the tomb to its new position. This is a long job, and will take two or three days at least.

July 9th. —9.00 p.m. Just at sunset we were startled by the howling of, seemingly, every dog in the village. It lasted for ten minutes or a quarter of an hour, and then ceased as suddenly as it began. This, and a curious mist that has risen round the church, makes me feel rather anxious about the "Sarah Tomb." According to the best-established traditions of the Vampire-haunted countries, the disturbance of dogs or wolves at sunset is supposed to indicate the presence of one of these fiends, and local fog is always considered to be a certain sign. The Vampire has the power of producing it for the purpose of concealing its movements near its hiding-place at any time.

I dare not mention or even hint my fears to the Rector, for he is, not unnaturally perhaps, a rank disbeliever in many things that I know, from experience, are not only possible but even probable. I must work this out alone at first, and get his aid without his knowing in what direction he is helping me. I shall now watch till midnight at least.

10.15 p.m. As I feared and half expected. Just before ten there was another outburst of the hideous howling. It was commenced most distinctly by a particularly horrible and blood-curdling wail from the vicinity of the churchyard. The chorus lasted only a few minutes, however, and at the end of it I saw a large dark shape, like a huge dog, emerge from the fog and lope away at a rapid canter towards the open country. Assuming this to be what I fear, I shall see it return soon after midnight.

12.30 p.m. I was right. Almost as midnight struck I saw the beast returning. It stopped at the spot where the fog seemed to commence, and lifting up its head, gave tongue to that particularly horrible long-drawn wail that I had noticed as preceding the outburst earlier in the evening.

Tomorrow I shall tell the Rector what I have seen; and if, as I expect, we hear of some neighbouring sheep-fold having been raided, I shall get him to watch with me for this nocturnal marauder. I shall also examine the "Sarah Tomb" for something which he may notice without any previous hint from me.

July 10th. I found the workmen this morning much disturbed in mind about the howling of the dogs. "We doan't like it, zur," one of them said to me—"we doan't like it; there was summat abroad last night that was unholy." They were still more uncomfortable when the news came round that a large dog had made a raid upon a flock of sheep, scattering them far and wide, and leaving three of them dead with torn throats in the field.

When I told the Rector of what I had seen and what was being said in the village, he immediately decided that we must try and catch or at least identify the beast I had seen. "Of course," said he, "it is some dog lately imported into the neighbourhood, for I know of nothing about here nearly as large as the animal you describe, though its size may be due to the deceptive moonlight."

This afternoon I asked the Rector, as a favour, to assist me in lifting the temporary cover that was on the tomb, giving as an excuse the reason that I wished to obtain a portion of the curious mortar with which it had been sealed. After a slight demur he consented, and we raised the lid. If the sight that met our eyes gave me a shock, at least it appalled Grant.

"Great God!" he exclaimed; "the woman is alive!"

And so it seemed for a moment. The corpse had lost much of its starved appearance and looked hideously fresh and alive. It was still wrinkled and shrunken, but the lips were firm, and of the rich red hue of health. The eyes, if possible, were more appalling than ever, though fixed and staring. At one corner of the mouth I thought I noticed a slight dark-coloured froth, but I said nothing about it then.

"Take your piece of mortar, Harry," gasped Grant, "and let us shut the tomb again. God help me! Parson though I am, such dead faces frighten me!"

Nor was I sorry to hide that terrible face again; but I got my bit of mortar, and I have advanced a step towards the solution of the mystery. This afternoon the tomb was moved several feet towards its new position, but it will be two or three days yet before we shall be ready to replace the slab.

10.15 p.m. Again the same howling at sunset, the same fog enveloping the church, and at ten o'clock the same great beast slipping silently out into the open country. I must get the Rector's help and watch for its return. But precautions we must take, for if things are as I believe, we take our lives in our hands when we venture out into the night to waylay the—*Vampire*. Why not admit it at once? For that the beast I have seen as the Vampire of that evil thing in the tomb I can have no reasonable doubt.

Not yet come to its full strength, thank Heaven! after the starvation of nearly two centuries, for at present it can only maraud as a wolf apparently. But, in a day or two, when full power returns, that dreadful woman in new strength and beauty will be able to leave her refuge. Then it would not be sheep merely that would satisfy her disgusting lust for blood, but victims that would yield their life-blood without a murmur to her caressing touch—victims that, dying of her foul embrace, themselves must become Vampires in their turn to prey on others.

Mercifully my knowledge gives me a safeguard; for that little piece of mortar that I rescued today from the tomb contains a portion of the Sacred Host, and who holds it, humbly and firmly believing in its virtue, may pass safely through such an ordeal as I intend to submit myself and the Rector to tonight.

12.30 p.m. Our adventure is over for the present, and we are back safe.

After writing the last entry recorded above, I went off to find Grant and tell him that the marauder was out on the prowl again. "But, Grant," I said, "before we start out tonight I must insist that you will let me prosecute this affair in my own way; you must promise to put yourself completely under my orders, without asking any questions as to the why and wherefore."

After a little demur, and some excusable chaff on his part at the serious view I was taking of what he called a "dog hunt," he gave me his promise. I then told him that we were to watch tonight and try and track the mysterious beast, but not to interfere with it in any way. I think, in spite of his jests, that I impressed him with the fact that there might be, after all, good reason for my precautions.

It was just after eleven when we stepped out into the still night.

Our first move was to try and penetrate the dense fog round the church, but there was something so chilly about it, and a faint smell so disgustingly rank and loathsome, that neither our nerves nor our stomachs were proof against it. Instead, we stationed ourselves in the dark shadow of a yew tree that commanded a good view of the wicket entrance to the churchyard.

At midnight the howling of the dogs began again, and in a few minutes we saw a large grey shape, with green eyes shining like lamps, shamble swiftly down the path towards us.

The Rector started forward, but I laid a firm hand upon his arm and whispered a warning "Remember!" Then we both stood very still and watched as the great beast cantered swiftly by. It was real enough, for we could hear the clicking of its nails on the stone flags. It passed within a few yards of us, and seemed to be nothing more nor less than a great grey wolf, thin and gaunt, with bristling hair and dripping jaws. It stopped where the mist commenced, and turned round. It was truly a horrible sight, and made one's blood run cold. The eyes burnt like fires, the upper lip was snarling and raised, showing the great canine teeth, while round the mouth hung and dripped a dark-coloured froth.

It raised its head and gave tongue to its long wailing howl, which was answered from afar by the village dogs. After standing for a few moments it turned and disappeared into the thickest part of the fog.

Very shortly afterwards the atmosphere began to clear, and within ten minutes the mist was all gone, the dogs in the village were silent, and the night seemed to reassume its normal aspect. We examined the spot where the beast had been standing and found, plainly enough upon the stone flags, dark spots of froth and saliva.

"Well, Rector," I said, "will you admit now, in view of the things you have seen today, in consideration of the legend, the woman in the tomb, the fog, the howling dogs, and, last but not least, the mysterious beast you have seen so close, that there is something not quite normal in it all? Will you put yourself unreservedly in my hands and help me, whatever I may do, to first make assurance doubly sure, and finally take the necessary steps for putting an end to this horror of the night?" I saw that the uncanny influence of the night was strong upon him, and wished to impress it as much as possible.

"Needs must," he replied, "when the Devil drives: and in the face of what I have seen I must believe that some unholy forces are at work. Yet, how can they work in the sacred precincts of a church? Shall we not call rather upon Heaven to assist us in our need."

"Grant," I said solemnly, "that we must do, each in his own way. God helps those who help themselves, and by His help and the light of my knowledge we must fight this battle for Him and the poor lost soul within."

We then returned to the rectory and to our rooms, though I have sat up to write this account while the scene is fresh in my mind.

July 11th. Found the workmen again very much disturbed in their minds, and full of a strange dog that had been seen during the night by several people, who had hunted it. Farmer Stotman, who had been watching his sheep (the same flock that had been raided the night before), had surprised it over a fresh carcass and tried to drive it off, but its size and fierceness so alarmed him that he had beaten a hasty retreat for a gun. When he returned the animal was gone, though he found that three more sheep from his flock were dead and torn.

The "Sarah Tomb" was moved today to its new position; but it was a long, heavy business, and there was not time to replace the covering slab. For this I was glad, as in the prosaic light of day the Rector almost disbelieves the events of the night, and is prepared to think everything to have been magnified and distorted by our imagination.

As, however, I could not possibly proceed with my war of extermination against this foul thing without assistance, and as there is nobody else I can rely upon, I appealed to him for one more night—to convince him that it was no delusion, but a ghastly, horrible truth, which must be fought and conquered for our own sakes, as well as that of all those living in the neighbourhood.

"Put yourself in my hands, Rector," I said, "for tonight at least. Let us take those precautions which my study of the subject tells me arc the right ones. Tonight you and I must watch in the church; and I feel assured that tomorrow you will be as convinced as I am, and be equally prepared to take those awful steps which I know to be proper, and I must warn you that we shall find a more startling change in the body lying there than you noticed yesterday."

My words came true; for on raising the wooden cover once more the rank stench of a slaughter-house arose, making us feel positively sick. There lay the Vampire, but how changed from the starved and shrunken corpse we saw two days ago for the first time! The wrinkles had almost disappeared, the flesh was firm and full, the crimson lips grinned horribly over the long pointed teeth, and a distinct smear of blood had trickled down one corner of the mouth. We set our teeth, however, and hardened our hearts. Then we replaced the cover and put what we had collected into a safe place in the vestry. Yet even now Grant could not believe that there was any real or pressing danger concealed in that awful tomb, as he raised strenuous objections to any apparent desecration of the body without further proof. This he shall have tonight. God grant that I am not taking too much on myself. If there is any truth in old legends it would be easy enough to destroy the Vampire now; but Grant will not have it.

I hope for the very best of this night's work, but the danger in waiting is very great.

6 p.m. I have prepared everything: the sharp knives, the pointed stake, fresh garlic, and the wild dog-roses. All these I have taken and concealed in the vestry, where we can get at them when our solemn vigil commences.

If either or both of us die with our fearful task undone, let those reading my record see that this is done. I lay it upon them as a solemn obligation. "That the Vampire be pierced through the heart with the stake, then let the Burial Service be read over the poor clay at last released from its doom. Thus shall the Vampire cease to be, and a lost soul rest."

July 12th. All is over. After the most terrible night of watching and horror one Vampire at least will trouble the world no more. But how thankful should we be to a merciful Providence that that awful tomb was not disturbed by anyone not having the knowledge necessary to deal with its dreadful occupant! I write this with no feelings of self-complacency, but simply with a great gratitude for the years of study I have been able to devote to this special subject.

And now to my tale.

Just before sunset last night the Rector and I locked ourselves into the church, and took up our position in the pulpit. It was one of those pulpits, to be found in some churches, which is entered from the vestry, the preacher appearing at a good height through an arched opening in the wall. This gave us a sense of security (which we felt we needed), a good view of the interior, and direct access to the implements which I had concealed in the vestry.

The sun set and the twilight gradually deepened and faded. There was, so far, no sign of the usual fog, nor any howling of the dogs. At nine o'clock the moon rose, and her pale light gradually flooded the aisles, and still no sign of any kind from the "Sarah Tomb." The Rector had asked me several times what he might expect, but I was determined that no words or thought of mine should influence him, and that he should be convinced by his own senses alone.

By half-past ten we were both getting very tired, and I began to think that perhaps after all we should see nothing that night. However, soon after eleven we observed a light mist rising from the "Sarah Tomb." It seemed to scintillate and sparkle as it rose, and curled in a sort of pillar or spiral.

I said nothing, but I heard the Rector give a sort of gasp as he clutched my arm feverishly. "Great Heaven!" he whispered, "it is taking shape."

And, true enough, in a very few moments we saw standing erect by the tomb the ghastly figure of the Countess Sarah!

She looked thin and haggard still, and her face was deadly white; but the crimson lips looked like a hideous gash in the pale cheeks, and her eyes glared like red coals in the gloom of the church.

It was a fearful thing to watch as she stepped unsteadily down the aisle, staggering a little as if from weakness and exhaustion. This was perhaps natural, as her body must have suffered much physically from her long incarceration, in spite of the unholy forces which kept it fresh and well.

We watched her to the door, and wondered what would happen; but it appeared to present no difficulty, for she melted through it and and disappeared.

"Now, Grant," I said, "do you believe?"

"Yes," he replied, "I must. Everything is in your hands, and I will obey your commands to the letter, if you can only instruct me how to rid my poor people of this unnameable terror."

"By God's help I will," said I; "but you shall be yet more convinced first, for we have a terrible work to do, and much to answer for in the future, before we leave the church again this morning. And now to work, for in its present weak state the Vampire will not wander far, but may return at any time, and must not find us unprepared."

We stepped down from the pulpit and, taking dog-roses and garlic from the vestry, proceeded to the tomb. I arrived first and, throwing off the wooden cover, cried, "Look! it is empty!" There was nothing there! Nothing except the impress of the body in the loose damp mould!

I took the flowers and laid them in a circle round the tomb, for legend teaches us that Vampires will not pass over these particular blossoms if they can avoid it.

Then, eight or ten feet away, I made a circle on the stone pavement. large enough for the Rector and myself to stand in, and within the circle I placed the implements that I had brought into the church with me.

"Now," I said, "from this circle, which nothing unholy can step across, you shall see the Vampire face to face, and see her afraid to cross that other circle of garlic and dog-roses to regain her unholy refuge. But on no account step beyond the holy place you stand in, for the Vampire has a fearful strength not her own, and, like a snake, can draw her victim willingly to his own destruction."

Now so far my work was done, and, calling the Rector, we stepped into the Holy Circle to await the Vampire's return.

Nor was this long delayed. Presently a damp, cold odour seemed to pervade the church, which made our hair bristle and flesh to creep. And then down the aisle with noiseless feet came That which we watched for.

I heard the Rector mutter a prayer, and I held him tightly by the arm, for he was shivering violently.

Long before we could distinguish the features we saw the glowing eyes and the crimson sensual mouth.

She went straight to her tomb, but stopped short when she encountered my flowers. She walked right round the tomb seeking a place to enter, and as she walked she saw us. A spasm of diabolical hate and fury passed over her face; but it quickly vanished, and a smile of love, more devilish still, took its place. She stretched out her arms towards us. Then we saw that round her mouth gathered a bloody froth, and from under her lips long pointed teeth gleamed and champed.

She spoke: a soft soothing voice, a voice that carried a spell with it, and affected us both strangely, particularly the Rector. I wished to test as far as possible, without endangering our lives, the Vampire's power.

Her voice had a soporific effect, which I resisted easily enough, but which seemed to throw the Rector into a sort of trance. More than this: it seemed to compel him to her in spite of his efforts to resist.

"Come!" she said—"come! I give sleep and peace—sleep and peace—sleep and peace."

She advanced a little towards us; but not far, for I noted that the Sacred Circle seemed to keep her back like an iron hand.

My companion seemed to become demoralized and spellbound. He tried to step forward and, finding me detain him, whispered, "Harry, let go! I must go! She is calling me! I must! I must! Oh, help me! help me!" And he began to struggle.

It was time to finish.

"Grant!" I cried, in a loud, firm voice, "in the name of all that you hold sacred, have done and play the man!"

He shuddered violently and gasped, "Where am I?" Then he remembered, and clung to me convulsively for a moment.

At this a look of damnable hate changed the smiling face before us, and with a sort of shriek she staggered back.

"Back!" I cried: "back to your unholy tomb! No longer shall you molest the suffering world! Your end is near."

It was fear that now showed itself in her beautiful face (for it was beautiful in spite of its horror) as she shrank back, back and over the circlet of flowers, shivering as she did so. At last, with a low mournful cry, she appeared to melt back again into her tomb.

As she did so the first gleams of the rising sun lit up the world, and I knew all danger was over for the day.

Taking Grant by the arm, I drew him with me out of the circle and led him to the tomb. There lay the Vampire once more, still in her living death as we had a moment before seen her in her devilish life. But in the eyes remained that awful expression of hate, and cringing, appalling fear.

Grant was pulling himself together.

"Now," I said, "will you dare the last terrible act and rid the world for ever of this horror?"

"By God!" he said solemnly, "I will. Tell me what to do."

"Help me to lift her out of her tomb. She can harm us no more," I replied.

With averted faces we set to our terrible task, and laid her out upon the flags.

"Now," I said, "read the Burial Service over the poor body, and then let us give it its release from this living hell that holds it." Reverently the Rector read the beautiful words, and reverently I made the necessary responses. When it was over I took the stake and, without giving myself time to think, plunged it with all my strength through the heart.

As though really alive, the body for a moment writhed and kicked convulsively, and an awful heart-rending shriek woke the silent church; then all was still.

Then we lifted the poor body back; and, thank God! the consolation that legend tells is never denied to those who have to do such awful work as ours came at last. Over the face stole a great and solemn peace; the lips lost their crimson hue, the prominent sharp teeth sank back into the mouth, and for a moment we saw before us the calm, pale face of a most beautiful woman, who smiled as she slept. A few minutes more, and she faded away to dust before our eyes as we watched. We set to work and cleaned up every trace of our work, and then departed for the rectory. Most thankful were we to step out of the church, with its horrible associations, into the rosy warmth of the summer morning.

With the above end the notes in my father's diary, though a few days later this further entry occurs:

July 15th. Since the 12th everything has been quiet and as usual. We replaced and sealed up the "Sarah Tomb" this morning. The workmen were surprised to find the body had disappeared, but took it to be the natural result of exposing it to the air.

One odd thing came to my ears today. It appears that the child of one of the villagers strayed from home the night of the 11th inst., and was found asleep in a coppice near the church, very pale and quite exhausted. There were two small marks on her throat, which have since disappeared.

What does this mean? I have, however, kept it to myself, as, now that the Vampire is no more, no further danger either to that child or any other is to be apprehended. It is only those who die of the Vampire's embrace that become Vampires at death in their turn.